FANTASTIC FAMILIES

Published in the UK by Scholastic, 2023
1 London Bridge, London, SE1 9BG
Scholastic Ireland, 89E Lagan Road, Dublin
Industrial Estate, Glasnevin, Dublin, D11 HP5F

SCHOLASTIC and associated logos are trademarks and/
or registered trademarks of Scholastic Inc.

Text © Omari McQueen, 2023
Illustrations by Sophia Green © Scholastic, 2023

The right of Omari McQueen to be identified as the author
of this work has been asserted by him in accordance
with the Copyright, Designs and Patents Act, 1988.

ISBN 978 0702 32396 6

A CIP catalogue record for this book is
available from the British Library.

Printed and bound in China by C&C
Offset Printing Co., Ltd.
Paper made from wood grown in sustainable
forests and other controlled sources.

2 4 6 8 10 9 7 5 3 1

www.scholastic.co.uk

FANTASTIC FAMILIES

OMARI MCQUEEN   Illustrated by SOPHIA GREEN

I LOVE MY FAMILY...

They make me feel **SO** happy!

Family love is like no other, and having
each other is all that matters.

Family will be there from the **VERY BEGINNING...**

until the very end.

It doesn't matter what size your family is,
it's the **LOVE** you have for them that counts.

FAMILIES ARE LIKE FOOD...

some **SPICY**...

some **SAVOURY**...

some SWEET...

but always the
MOST DELICIOUS DISH!

Family is my favourite

PROTECTIVE BLANKET...

I always feel so safe in my parents' arms.

Wherever I travel to, there
is no place like home...

I LOVE
MY FAMILY!

My family are like **BOWLING PINS...**

we can get knocked down but we will
ALWAYS stand together again!

To be a family
is to be a **TEAM**.

With your family by your
side, you're sure to **WIN**.

Family is the **FIRST GIFT** you open and **ONE YOU WILL NEVER FORGET.**

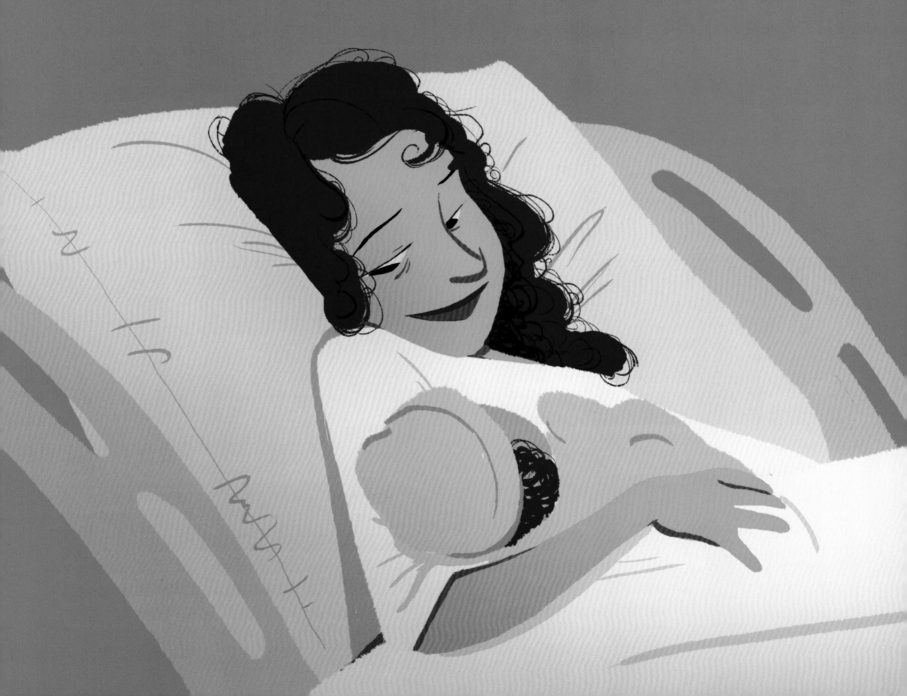

My **GREATEST TREASURE** is my family...

and sharing experiences with them
makes everything that much more **SPECIAL**.

A house just isn't a home without family...
and my favourite song is the sound of my home.
The time you spend with your family is worth every second...

I LOVE MY FAMILY!

Sticks and stones can break my bones,
but my family is always there to
pick me up when I'm feeling down.

Family means **NO ONE** will be
left behind or forgotten.

The strength of a **UNITED FAMILY** is like no other...

they can give you **POWER** in times of need...

look after **YOU** when you're feeling unwell...

and **LOVE** and **SUPPORT** you always.

My family means the **WORLD** to me!

Your family has just the right **INGREDIENTS** for the **PERFECT RECIPE!**

There is nothing more important
than the people you have at home...

I LOVE MY FAMILY!

My family puts a smile on
my face because...

MY FAMILY LOVES ME FOR ME!

Time is **FREE** but **PRICELESS** when spent with family.

The **MEMORIES** I make with my family mean **EVERYTHING** to me!

Family is where
your life begins...

AND THE
LOVE NEVER ENDS.

I LOVE
MY FAMILY!

COOKIE DOUGH CHOCOLATE CUPS

WHAT YOU NEED:

CUPS

- 440g mini vegan chocolate chips
- 2 tablespoons coconut oil

Always ask an adult before starting to bake these cookie dough cups!

COOKIE DOUGH

- 170g mini vegan chocolate chips
- 110g light brown sugar
- 3 tablespoons coconut oil
- 2 tablespoons almond milk
- 100g almond flour
- 130g oat flour
- 1 teaspoon vanilla extract
- ½ teaspoon salt
- Sprinkles

- Silicone cupcake moulds or cupcake tin lined with clingfilm

MAKES 12

PREP time 1 hour

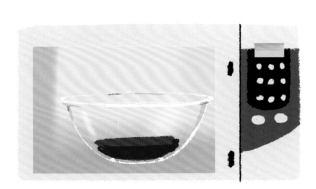

1 Place the mini vegan chocolate chips into a glass bowl with the coconut oil and heat in the microwave for 30 seconds at a time (stirring between each interval) until fully melted.

2 Add 2 tablespoons of the melted chocolate mix into each cupcake case, moving the mould around to so that it's fully covered. Place the moulds in the fridge to set for 10–15 minutes.

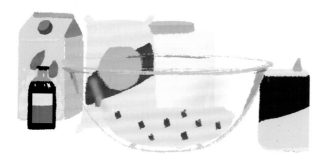

3 Meanwhile, to make the cookie dough, mix together the brown sugar, coconut oil, almond milk and vanilla extract. Then add the oat flour, almond flour, chocolate chips and salt and mix all the ingredients together until you get a dough-like consistency.

4 Roll the cookie dough into 12 small balls and place them inside the chocolate cases.

5 Pour the remaining melted chocolate from step 1 into each cookie cup until the cookie dough is covered and the cup is full to the top.

6 Add the sprinkles on top of each cup and leave to set in the fridge until the chocolate has solidified. **ENJOY!**

QUESTIONS TO THINK ABOUT WITH YOUR FANTASTIC FAMILY

Families come in all shapes and sizes.

Who makes up your family?

People in families can be very similar to each

other but they can also be very different!

What are the similarities and differences in your family?